PLAY by PLAY

NEW YORK TIMES BESTSELLING AUTHOR
KAYLEE RYAN

PLAY BY PLAY
Copyright © 2020 Kaylee Ryan

All Rights Reserved.
This book may not be reproduced in any manner whatsoever without the written permission of Kaylee Ryan, except for the use of brief quotations in articles and or reviews.

This book is a work of fiction. Names, characters, events, locations, businesses and plot are products of the author's imagination and meant to be used in a fictitious manner. Any resemblance to actual persons, living or dead, or actual events throughout the story are purely coincidental. The author acknowledges trademark owners and trademarked status of various products referenced in this work of fiction, which have been used without permission. The publication and use of these trademarks are not authorized, sponsored or associated by or with the trademark owners.

The following story contains sexual situations and strong language. It is intended for adult readers.

Cover Design: Lori Jackson Design
Cover Photography: Reggie Deanching
Model: Quinn Biddle
Editing: Hot Tree Editing
Proofreading: Deaton Author Services
Paperback Formatting: Integrity Formatting

CHAPTER ONE
Jase

HAVE YOU EVER done something accidentally on purpose? You know, pretend that you "accidentally" forgot to complete a task, when the truth is that you didn't want to do it or didn't have time? I guess that's also called a little white lie. However you want to refer to it, I just committed the crime.

She left me no choice.

For over a year, I've been asking Samantha Wilson to go out on a date with me. Every time she turns me down. Although her words say no, I can see it in her eyes, she wants to. She's stuck on this concept that I'm a player. Sure, I played the game on and off the field. Now that I'm retired, I'm ready for more. I want to settle down, and Samantha claims she doesn't believe me.

I call bullshit.

She wants me, but she's fighting it. I'm just a regular guy. I know it's the fame that scares her. If she could only look past that to see the man, we'd be dating if not married by now. Yes, I know that's a big assumption, but it's also a big deal that she's all I can think about.

I can still remember the day I first laid eyes on her. I had just announced my retirement from the NFL and had moved back home to Nashville. I was born and raised in Ohio, but my sister married a musician, and once she started having babies, Mom and Dad couldn't stand the distance. They moved here soon after. I love the city and being close to my family. As soon as I announced my retirement, I put my house in Texas up for sale and headed home. Once I was settled in, it was time to connect with some old friends. Royce Riggins and I went to college together and stayed in touch through the years. I called him once I was settled, and we set up a time to have lunch.

That's when I saw her. *My Sam.* With her long brown hair and those big brown eyes, she captured my attention immediately. And although she thinks I'm playing, I'm not. Sure, in the beginning, it was me seeing a beautiful woman and wanting the pleasure of her company. Now, it's more than that. So much more.

That brings us to now. I stopped by Royce's office earlier and purposely left my cell phone on the chair in his office. I wanted it to look as though it fell out of my pocket. The crime I told you about? That was my phone call to his office from my landline asking if I left my phone. Of course, he found it and insisted his assistant—my Sam—could drop it off. Apparently, she was dropping off some contracts and would be in the neighborhood. I knew all of this. He told me already, hence the reason I left my phone, hoping like hell this was how it would play out.

The buzzer sounds, letting me know that someone is at the gate. *Showtime.* "Yes?" I say into the intercom. I send up a silent prayer that my sister and brother-in-law Kacen aren't outside in their yard to hear this go down. I bought a house on their street, along with the rest of the guys in Kacen's band. It's like our own little village. Kacen will never cease to give me shit over the beautiful woman who spent time at my place. Not that I really care. He was the same way when it came to my sister, Logan. He loves her fiercely and makes no apologies for it.

"Hey, player." Sam's voice cracks over the line. "I've got your phone."

"Thank you," I tell her, buzzing her through. I don't waste time as I rush to the door to greet her. "There she is." I smile as she climbs out of her car. Her long tan legs are in a gray pencil skirt that has me thinking about what it would feel like to have them wrapped around my head while I—

Her voice interrupts my thoughts.

"Earth to Jase." She laughs, and the sound grips around my heart. "I lost you there for a minute." She takes three more steps, and she's standing in front of me. "Here's your phone. You know, you might want to keep a better eye on this thing, player. Losing it will surely interfere with your hook-up game," she teases.

"Samantha." I shake my head. "How many times do I have to tell you, there is no hooking up. I'm waiting for you."

"Yeah, yeah." The smile on her face as she shakes her head in disbelief tells me she thinks I'm teasing.

"I can prove it."

"Yeah? How?"

"Come inside."

"Oh, no." She chuckles. "I'm not falling for the 'come inside so I can seduce you' play. I thought you had more game than that, Andrews."

Frustrating woman. "Let me show you."

Her eyes stray to my cock that's hard and getting harder by the second with her eyes on me. "I'm..." She swallows hard. "I'm good."

"Samantha." I reach out, placing my finger under her chin, lifting her gaze to mine. "Please? I promise I'll be on my best behavior. I have something to show you, and before you spout off something about my cock, that's not it. Please, let me show you, and if you want to leave after that, I'll let you go without a complaint." For tonight that is. I'm not giving up on her that easily. I know without a doubt she's the one for me.

"Jase," she says with a sigh.

She's wavering. Sliding my hand into hers, I hold her gaze. "Come with me." I stare into her big brown eyes, willing her to trust me.

"Five minutes," she relents. "I'll come inside for five minutes." Her voice is stern and settled, but once she sees what I have in store for her, I'm hoping she'll change her mind.

"Thank you, beautiful." I lean in and kiss her cheek. "Follow me." With her hand still clasped tightly in mine, I lead her into my house. This isn't the first time she's been here. I've had get-togethers and insisted that Royce get her here, no matter what he had to do. She's been in my home, but never just the two of us. "Close your eyes," I say once we're inside.

"Jase—" She starts, but I stop her with another kiss. This time to the corner of her mouth.

"Please, Sam. Trust me." I give her hand a soft squeeze, willing her to do just that.

She nods. "Okay." Her voice is soft, and I know she's worried, but she doesn't need to be. Never with me. Her eyes slide closed, and my heart swells. I'm finally making progress with her.

Moving to stand behind her, I push her long locks to one shoulder and place my hands on her hips. "I'm right here," I whisper in her ear. She shivers at the contact, and my smile grows. "Over a year, Samantha... I've wanted you for over a year." I keep my voice soft as we walk as one into the living room. "You ready for your surprise, baby?" I ask her. This time I place a soft kiss just under her ear.

"Y-Yes," she murmurs.

"Open your eyes, Samantha."

She sucks in a breath as she takes in the sight before her. "W-What is this?"

"This is our first date."

"What?" she breathes.

I tighten my arms around her. "You're right about me in one aspect. I am a player." She stiffens in my arms. "Football was my life from the time I was old enough to hold a ball, and it's still a huge part of who I am, even though I'm retired. I'm playing, beautiful, but I always play to win."

"What exactly are you planning to win?" she asks, turning her head to look at me from over her shoulder.

"You. Your heart." I push back a strand of hair that has fallen over her eyes. "This isn't a game, but this is my hail Mary to win you over. Have dinner with me?" I say, nodding to the picnic I've arranged on my living room floor.

"I can't believe you did all of this. How did you—?" She stops. "You didn't accidentally leave your phone at the office, did you?"

"Nope." I wink at her. "I'm willing to do whatever it takes to get time with you."

"What are we having?" she asks, turning her gaze back to the living room.

"Chicken salad sandwiches, fresh fruit, and turtle cheesecake for dessert."

"How did you—?" she starts and stops.

"I know you, Sam. I've watched you for months, memorizing every detail. I know you love chicken salad from Sanderson's market. I know that fresh strawberries and grapes are your favorites, and I know that turtle cheesecake is your indulgence."

"Jase." My name is a whisper from her lips.

"Yeah, baby?"

"I—" She shakes her head.

Moving to stand in front of her, I place my hands on either side of her face. Brown eyes meet blue as I hold her gaze—willing her to say yes. "Samantha, will you allow me the honor of your company and have dinner with me?"

"So formal," she teases, a blinding smile lighting up her face.

"I'm not ashamed to admit I'm pulling out the big guns."

She nods. "Yes, I'll have dinner with you."

"Thank fuck," I mumble, placing a kiss to her forehead. I lead her to the picnic area I have set up in the middle of my living room floor. She puts her hand on my shoulder for balance as she removes her black heels, and hikes up her skirt to step up on the platform I've created. Not wearing shoes, I step up next to her and take her hand helping her sit, then take the spot next to her, and begin to unpack the picnic basket. I notice there is a slight tremble in my hands. I've played football in front of millions of people. There are pictures of me in nothing but my tight-as-fuck boxer briefs on billboards across the United States, and none of that made me the least bit nervous. Sitting next to a beautiful woman, one who's done nothing but consume my mind for the last year, makes me nervous. She's giving me an opening, and I don't want to mess this up.

CHAPTER TWO
Samantha

I'VE ENTERED AN alternate universe. That's the only explanation for my current situation. I admit I was excited when Royce asked me to stop by Jase's house and deliver his phone that he left in Royce's office. Jase Andrews is every woman's fantasy. At six foot five, with sexy brown hair that you want to run your fingers through, and those blue eyes, it's all enough to have panties dropping. Add the fact that he still works out and his body is a masterpiece... he has women falling all over him.

I can still remember the first time I ever saw him shirtless. Royce's parents had a Fourth of July party. I brought my best friend, Carrie. Royce's younger brother Marshall met us at the house and drove us to the lake in his truck. As soon as I stepped out of the truck, Jase was there, shirtless and in nothing but a pair of board shorts. If it hadn't been for Carrie, I would have fallen ass over heels making a fool of myself. My bestie had my back as she steered me over toward Lena Riggins, Royce's mom. We helped her get the food together, which gave my body time to cool down and for me to get myself in check.

He's a huge flirt, and a player on and off the field, something he rightfully admitted. He claims he's different now, that I'm different for him. I've heard him tell me that hundreds of times in the last year, but this… this moment is different from all the times before. He's not acting like the flirty teasing player I've known him to be. Today he's something… more.

"Is this turf?" I ask, taking a seat on the blanket spread out on his living room floor.

"Yep. We can't have a picnic without grass, and it's too cold outside for a picnic, so I improvised."

"Improvised? Jase, there is a huge platform in the middle of your living room covered in turf. There are clouds hanging from your ceiling that I'm pretty sure wasn't blue the last time I was here." I take in the room and am in awe at the effort he's put into this. The wooden platform is covered in turf. There is a small tree in a huge flowerpot, and smaller pots of flowers sitting off to the side.

In the center is a quilt and a picnic basket. The clouds hanging overhead are incredible. "Are those lights?" I ask, tilting my head back to take them in.

"Yes."

"You painted your ceiling?"

"Yes."

"I can't believe you did all this." I shake my head as I try to comprehend his efforts.

"This is our first date, Sam. That means something. I wanted it to be a moment that neither of us would ever forget."

"The player makes a play," I mumble.

"First things first," he says, reaching behind him and grabbing a small cooler. He flips the top and pulls out a bottle of root beer. Not the plastic bottles. No, these are the old-time glass bottles that are hard to find. "This is your favorite, right?" he asks, using a bottle opener to flip off the cap.

"H-How did you know that?" I ask, taking the bottle from his hand.

"You said it once. I don't know where we were, but I remember you saying that you loved them as a kid, and it was your favorite, but you didn't see them in stores often," he explains.

"I don't know what to say to that," I confess.

"Say thank you, Jase." He grins. "Now, for the main course." He reaches back into the coolers and pulls out two sandwich bags containing what I assume are chicken salad sandwiches. "Now, take it easy on me. This is my first time making this. I tasted it, but a chef I am not. I made sure to add almonds and red grapes. That's how you like it, right?"

"Are you stalking me?" I ask, my voice rising an octave. I have no idea how in the hell he knows all of this about me.

I expect him to laugh or crack a joke, but neither happens. "No, baby, I'm not stalking you. Do I pay attention where you're concerned? You're damn right, I do."

I have no words. Anyone who knows me knows that's not me. Jase Andrews has effectively rendered me speechless.

"And this—" He reaches back into the cooler, producing a glass container with a plastic lid. "Fresh fruit. I made sure to get extra strawberries and grapes," he says, pulling the lid off the container and placing it on the blanket in front of us. "I have dip too," he says, and his dimples wink at me.

"This is a lot of work for sex," I blurt. It's cruel, and I regret the words as soon as they leave my mouth.

"Samantha," he sighs. "This isn't about that. I want to date you. I want to spend time with you. Does that count time in my bed? Sure. But that's not all that this is. Surely, you can see that?"

"I'm sorry. That was uncalled for. I just can't seem to wrap my head around what you see in me. You can have any woman you want, yet you're chasing me."

"You're the only one I want," he says, his blue eyes boring into mine. His cell phone rings, and he ignores it.

"You gonna get that?" I ask.

He sighs, pulls his phone out of his pocket, and hits Ignore before tossing it across the room where it lands on the couch. "There is nothing more important than spending time with you."

"You make it hard to resist you when you say things like that." His words melt me, and I want to believe him, but it's hard for me to wrap my head around the fact that Jase Andrews wants me. I'm just me.

"Good." He leans in close. "I don't want you to resist me."

I don't want to resist him either, but I also need to feel as though he's giving me his attention for the right reasons. "Why me, Jase? I don't understand."

"You're the most beautiful woman I've ever laid eyes on. You're funny as hell, and I know without a doubt you'll be a partner. I want someone not afraid to call me on my shit. I also know that if I ever get this"—he places his hand over my heart—"it will be because of love, not the number of zeros in my bank account."

I close the distance and press my lips to his. Acting fully on instinct and the way the man makes my heart hammer in my chest. Our lips touch and goose bumps break out across my skin, just like every other time he's near.

Jase breaks the kiss, resting his forehead against

mine. "Does this mean you're going to stop fighting me?" he asks softly.

"I'm not sure."

Jase chuckles, his hot breath fanning against my face. "I'm not giving up, Sam."

"I don't think I want you to."

"Good." He places a chaste kiss to my lips. "Now, I think I promised you dinner." Pulling away, he reaches into the picnic basket and removes paper plates and napkins and gets to work unwrapping our sandwiches and placing them, and a hefty amount of fruit, on our plates. "Oh, I almost forgot." His arm disappears back into the basket, and he produces a bag of Garden Salsa SUNCHIPS, which are also my favorite.

"Thank you, Jase," I say when he offers me a plate.

"Tell me about your day." He settles back on the blanket and begins to eat, and I begin to tell him about my day. This is a side of Jase I've never seen before. Then again, maybe I've just been too blind to see. I've turned him down more times than I can count to protect my heart. After tonight, I don't know if that's possible anymore. He went beyond my wildest expectations and made this night special. He didn't even know if I would end up here with his phone. He did all of this on the chance that tonight would work out the way he hoped it would. Not only did he convince me to have our first date, but he stole a little piece of my heart too.

"Thank you for tonight," I say as he walks me to

the door a few hours later. The stars are shining bright in the night sky. I didn't realize how long I was here, but once we started talking, time just seemed to pass in a blur. We have more in common than I ever realized. We have the same taste in music. I also grew up watching football with my dad, making conversation easy. And tonight, there was nowhere that I would have rather been.

"When can we do it again?" he asks, stopping in his foyer.

"This is going to be hard to top." I smile up at him.

"Is that a challenge?" he asks.

"No. I don't need the theatrics. Just the pleasure of your company."

"When?" Jase asks, his voice husky as he leans in close.

"Whenever you're ready," I confess. I had such a good time with him tonight, and I'm tired of fighting this connection we have. It's too late anyway. My heart is already invested. I'll just have to deal with the pain if this doesn't work out.

"Tomorrow night?" He's quick to ask.

"Tomorrow is the Christmas party at Lena and Stanley's. She'd never forgive me if I missed it."

"Shit, I forgot about that. I'll pick you up."

I don't say anything to that. Instead, I think about how it's going to look showing up at my boss's family's Christmas party with his best friend. Royce can be broody at times, and I don't want me being there with Jase to cause problems.

"I'll handle Royce," Jase says, reading my mind. "I'll be at your place around five thirty." He leans in and kisses me softly. "Give me your keys. I'll go start your car while you're putting your coat on."

"You don't have to do that. It will warm up quickly."

"I know I don't have to. I want to." He reaches out and runs his index finger down my cheek. "I want to take care of you."

I don't know what to say, so I hand him my keys, and he grins. Sliding into my coat, I let the night wash over me, considering the last few hours. It's funny how things can change in the blink of an eye.

"All set?" he asks, coming back into the house.

"Yes." I stare up at him as he wraps his arms around me, pulling me into a hug.

"How'd I do?" he asks.

"Not bad for a player."

"Yeah? Well, lucky for you, my playbook is full."

I throw my head back and laugh. "I have no doubt, Jase Andrews. Of that, I have no doubt."

"Come on. I'll walk you out." He leads me to my car with his hand clasped in mine. "Text me when you get home?"

"Okay."

"Drive safe, babe." He kisses me one more time, just a soft press of his lips against mine before opening my door for me.

As I drive away, I glance in the rearview mirror. My face is lit with a smile, and then there's Jase.

Standing with his arms crossed over his chest, he watches me drive away. My smile grows.

What started as a favor to my boss turned into a night I will never forget.

CHAPTER THREE

Jase

I'M FIFTEEN MINUTES early. I couldn't stand another minute staring at the clock watching as each minute slowly ticked by. I needed to see her. So, here I am. Climbing out of my SUV and making my way to her front door. I raise my hand to knock, but the door swings open before I get a chance to.

"This another play in your book? Impress me by being early?"

I smile at the beauty before me. She's wearing a sweater, with black leggings. Her hair hangs down around her shoulders, and she literally takes my breath away. "No," I tell her honestly. "But I wanted to give you time to put these in water, and for us to not be late." I hand her the bouquet of flowers I've been holding behind my back.

Her eyes soften. "Well played." She grins, taking the offered bouquet and smelling them. "Thank you, Jase." She steps back. "Come on in while I put them in water."

This is the first time I've ever been to her place. I should be taking this opportunity to look around to learn more about her, but I can't tear my eyes away from her. I've wanted Sam for so long, and for the first time in over a year, I feel as though we might be making some progress.

"Ready?" she asks, walking toward me.

"Almost." When she's within reaching distance, I snake my arm around her waist and pull her into my chest. "Just need to do one thing first," I say before my lips descend on hers. The kiss is slow and sweet, but it lights a need inside me all the same. "Now, we can go," I say, forcing myself to pull my lips from hers.

"Yeah," she says, "we should do that." She tries to step out of my hold, but that won't do.

"Do you have everything you need?" I ask.

"Yes, I just have a box by the door I need to take with us."

"What's in the box?"

"A poinsettia for Lena, and a bottle of bourbon for Stanley."

"You trying to make me look bad, baby?" I ask.

She shrugs. "I still need to fill out the cards. I can add your name to them."

"You ready for the meaning of that?"

"I don't know," she replies as I bend and lift the box into my arms. "When you're ready, you let me know." Shifting the box to one arm, I lace my fingers with hers and step outside. I wait for Sam to lock the door before guiding her to my SUV. I left it running so it would be warm. I quickly open the back door and place the box inside, before moving to open her door for her.

"You know, you don't need to do all of this to impress me."

"Do all of what?" I ask, confused.

"The flowers, carrying boxes, opening doors. I already agreed to go with you."

Nodding for her to climb in the SUV, she does as I ask. Quickly, I shut the door to ward off the chill of the evening air and race around the front. Once I'm inside, I turn to look at the woman who has captured my attention. "I'm not trying to impress you, Samantha. I'm trying to treat you like you deserve to be treated. I know you don't have a very high opinion of me, but I'm more than some dumb jock who plays on and off the field. I'm a man who desires your company. That's it. This is me. It's who I am. You'll have to learn to take it or leave it." I hate that I'm being harsh with her, but I don't know what it's going to take to prove to her that this is real.

Strapping on my seat belt, I back out of her drive. Neither of us speaks a word until the home of my best friend's parents, Lena and Stanley Riggins comes into our view.

"I'm sorry," we say at the same time.

She reaches over and places her hand on my arm. "I'm sorry, Jase. I'm being unfair. This is just... surreal to me that you, Jase Andrews, want to be with me."

"Sam, I've been trying to get you to go on a date with me for over a year. How is this a surprise?"

She closes her eyes and takes a deep breath. "I never once thought you were being serious. I thought it was just another play for you to execute. That you were simply trying to convince the girl who turns you down to say yes. I'm sorry," she says again. "You did nothing to deserve that and to be honest, I have reason to think that way. I've let the fact that you're a professional football player, or were, get to my head."

"Why?"

"I just didn't think that a man like you, dripping with sex appeal, would want a woman like me. I'm nothing like the models or other celebrities I've seen on your arm."

"Dates. Those were dates. You're so much more than that." I knew she was attracted to me and her words confirm it, but I want us to be about more than that. Yes, I'm insanely attracted to her, but it's not just her body I want. I want all of her.

She nods and holds her hand out to me. I take it, not taking my eyes off hers. "My name is Samantha Wilson, and it's nice to meet you."

I grin when I catch on to what she's doing. Bending my head, I kiss the back of her hand that's still encased in mine. "Jase Andrews, the pleasure is all mine."

"Lord have mercy. I'm never going to survive you," she says, fanning her face with her free hand.

I don't even try to hold in my laughter. "Come on, you. Let's get this party started." Turning off the ignition, I grab the box, and together, we make our way inside.

We've been here twenty minutes, and Sam's already left me. She insisted that she help Lena in the kitchen, which is why I'm standing in the living room by the fireplace. It's the best place in the house where I have a clear view of the kitchen, as well as the room around me. I can talk to those who want to relive their football glory days by chatting with me while keeping an eye on Sam at the same time. I don't think she's going to disappear or try to leave without me. I just… like to watch her. She's gorgeous, and her smile and kind, loving heart just makes her more endearing to me.

"Is there a reason your eyes are tracking my assistant like a fucking hunter?" my best friend, and Sam's boss, Royce, says, pulling my attention away from my girl.

"She's my date."

"What do you mean, she's your date?"

"I mean, I bought her flowers, and picked her up and drove her here."

"So, she finally said yes?" He pauses, and I see it when the light bulb turns on in his head. "You better not be playing games with her. She's been with me since I started. I'd hate to have to cut you loose to keep her."

"Are you telling me after years of friendship, I'd get voted off the island if things don't work out between us?"

"Yes." There is no hesitation or remorse in his tone. "I trust her, and you know how hard that is for me with the shit 'she who shall not be named' did to me. I refuse to go through training a new assistant."

"Well, my *dear friend*, you're in luck. I don't plan on us not working out."

"Fuck me," he grumbles. "Why her? Why did you have to insist on going after my assistant?"

"What did you do this time, Jase?" Owen, Royce's brother, one of the four of them, joins the conversation. "The vein in his forehead looks like it's ready to burst."

"He's dating Sam," Royce says accusingly.

Owen nods. "She's a good one. Congrats, my man."

"See, why can't you be more like Owen? Where is your acceptance?" I ask Royce, pretending to be offended. I'm not. Not in the slightest. He's never known me to be serious or settle down. He does, however, know me well enough to understand that I'm a man of my word.

"What are we accepting?" Grant, another one of Royce's brothers, asks.

"Wait," Marshall, the youngest brother, says as he and Conrad, another brother, joins us.

"What is this, a family reunion?" I ask, giving them shit. There are five brothers in total, Royce being the oldest. As CEO, he takes his responsibility as a leader seriously. Each of his brothers also plays an important role at Riggins Enterprises, but Royce always seems to have the weight of the world on his shoulders. I miss the fun-loving guy from our college days. I know it's not the job, but more his ex that is to blame for this new version of him.

"We want the dirt," Marshall says, ignoring my comment.

"Spill it," Conrad adds.

As the youngest two brothers of the clan, they're the most outgoing as well. "Sam and I are together," I say with a shrug, taking a drink of my beer.

"Whoa whoa whoa, you said that you were on a date, not that the two of you were together." Royce glares at me.

"She's mine."

"Damn." Grant whistles. "Pulling out the big guns, Andrews."

Grant's the middle brother, just four years younger than Royce and me. He and Owen, who is two years younger, hung around us the most. However, if we were here, hanging out at the lake, all five of them were around, and their parents too.

Stanley and Lena Riggins built an oasis that they knew would always bring their sons home. To this day, we all still get together to hang out on the lake Stanley built when the boys were little.

"Just telling it like it is," I reply.

"Does she know that?" Owen asks.

My eyes seek her out to find her watching me. I smile at her, and she gives me a small wave before turning back to the tray of cookies in her hands. "Yeah, she knows."

"Son of a bitch," Royce mutters.

"Better watch it there, big guy. He looks pissed," Conrad says with no real warning in his tone. "Although, I think you can take him," he tells me.

"Thanks for the vote of confidence, brat." Royce shakes his head.

"Hey, the man has been laid out by men double your size for the entirety of his career. And he's built like a tank."

"Hey, my men kept me guarded," I tell him, defending my offensive linemen.

"Still, I think you've got this one," Marshall agrees.

"Enough," Royce snaps. "If you cause me to lose my assistant, I'll be kicking your ass."

I smirk. "If you think you can, not that we're ever going to have to find out. She and I are together."

"Yo, Samantha!" Conrad calls out. I watch as my girl turns her head. When she sees Conrad motioning her over, uncertainty crosses her expression. "We need you for a minute," he calls out as she starts this way.

My heart stutters in my chest as she grows near. Once she's within reaching distance, I step away from the wall and wrap my arms around her. "Missed you," I whisper in her ear. Her face turns a beautiful shade of light pink, and I can't help but wonder if her entire body is flushed as well.

"We should've placed bets," Marshall mutters under his breath.

"And give Andrews our money? No thanks," Owen chimes in.

"Sam," Royce whines. "Please tell me it's not true." His voice is pleading.

"What's not true?" she asks him.

"You and this guy?" He points to me.

"I thought he was your best friend."

"He is."

She glances over at me where I stand with my arm still wrapped around her waist. I give her a subtle nod. "He is a good kisser," she says. The chaos of four laughing Riggins brothers takes over the growling of one. I squeeze her hip, hoping to convey how happy her reply made me.

"You." Royce points his finger at me. "If you run her off, we're going to have words, Andrews."

"No one is going to run me off. I love my job, and I'm good at it." My Sam gives Royce a pointed look. If she's looking for denial, she's not going to get it. Not from Royce, or the other four brothers. She provides administrative support to all of them, so they're not going to say a word. They've stated more times than I can count how good she is at her job, how she keeps them all in line and on track. She spends most of her time working for Royce, but the others sing her praises as well.

Surprising me, she turns her back to the Riggins brothers and gives me all her attention. "I'm going to go finish helping Lena. Save me a seat at the table." She stands on her tiptoes, presses a kiss to the corner of my mouth, and saunters off.

"I'm going to marry her." I don't care who hears my declaration. I won't stop fighting until I win her heart.

CHAPTER FOUR
Samantha

I'M WALKING ON cloud nine. This weekend was nothing short of magical. For every time that Jase would ask me out, a new fantasy of what that would look like would appear in my head. Fantasy has nothing on reality. He's sweet and thoughtful and attentive—all things I never imagined him to be. In fact, most of my fantasies ended up with us in his bed, or against the wall, in the shower, all sans clothes.

"Morning, Samantha," Owen says as he walks past my desk. "Andrews treating you right?" he inquires.

"Yes." I give him the blinding smile that I can't seem to wipe off my face.

He nods. "You let me know if that changes," he says, moving on down the hall to his office. That's Owen for you. He's the quiet, stoic one. But I have no doubt that if Jase were to treat me wrong, and Owen found out about it, he wouldn't hesitate to throw a punch or two if necessary. It's the quiet ones you have to worry about.

Grant, Marshall, and Conrad all arrive for the day while I'm pulling voice mails off my phone. I've barely got the receiver back in the cradle when Royce appears before me. "Sam," he greets me.

"Mr. Riggins." I give him a big cheesy smile, and the corner of his lips twitch. "What can I do for you this morning?"

"The punch list for the Idaho location was supposed to be completed yesterday. Can you follow up with the contractor and get a status for me?"

"They called late last night. He said it's all complete and told you to call if you have any questions." I hand him the slip of paper with the details from the voice mail. "Your ten o'clock canceled and they didn't have a reason other than they were not ready, so I pushed them off to next month for a reschedule date."

"Thank you." He nods, going through the other messages I handed him. "You like that ogre of mine best friend?" he inquires.

"Yeah, Royce, I really do." He mumbles

something under his breath and walks off to his office. Not that I expected anything less from Royce Riggins. He's broody pretty much all the time. When I first started at Riggins Enterprises, he was different. Still broody at the office, but not so serious, or sad. His ex-wife really did a number on him. He needs to put himself out there and find love again, but he's stubborn as hell and convinced himself that a woman in his life is the last thing he needs.

"Hey, Sammy." Marshall grins, leaning against my desk. "I sent you an email with the marketing campaign for Idaho. Do you mind printing and binding ten copies?" he asks.

"Not at all. I'll get it done for you today."

"I don't need it until later in the week, so there's no rush." He stands to his full height. "Thank you." He waves as he walks toward the elevator. No doubt he's headed downstairs to the marketing department to touch base with his staff. That's one thing I will say about the Riggins brothers. None of them have to work, but they do, and they give it one hundred and ten percent.

I've worked all morning on a staffing report for Grant. Finally, it's finished, so I print it out and take it to his office. "Here you go," I say, stepping inside and placing it in his inbox. "Numbers look good this month." I smile at him.

"Thanks for doing that, Sam. I've been a little nuts with Idaho opening."

"That's my job, Grant. You don't have to thank me."

"Yes, I do." He grabs the report and thumbs through it. "You saved me some late nights. I appreciate you so much."

"Just remember that when it comes time for the broody one to give me my annual evaluation," I joke.

"I got your back, Wilson." His laughter follows me out of his office.

"There she is," a voice I would now recognize anywhere says as I come around the corner approaching my desk.

"Jase." I can hear the smile in my voice. "What are you doing here?"

He snakes an arm around my waist and kisses my cheek. "I came to take my girl to lunch."

"Don't you have somewhere else to be?" Royce grumbles, stepping out of his office. "Sam, I'm heading out for lunch then going to my meeting across town. I'll be back later this afternoon."

"Sure thing."

He glares at Jase. "Remember what I said," he warns, stepping past us.

"Good to see you too, sweetheart," Jase calls after him.

"Stop." I laugh, smacking lightly at his chest.

He shrugs. "You ready to go grab something to eat?"

"I packed my lunch today."

"It'll keep. We're going out."

"I only have an hour."

"I have an in with the boss man." He winks.

"Oh, no. He's pissy enough as it is. I'm not taking advantage of the fact that you're his best friend. If we can't go and be back in an hour, I'm not going." I step out of his hold and cross my arms over my chest.

"Fine, ball buster." He grins. "I'll have you back in an hour."

"Thank you, player." I smile sweetly at him before setting the alarm that won't allow anyone on the floor unless they have the code until I get back. There are only a handful of people who have the code, and the majority of them have the last name Riggins.

"So, where are we going?" I ask as we step outside of the building onto the busy sidewalk.

"Well, since my girl has given me strict instructions that she needs to be back at her desk in an hour, how about the deli?" He points to a small deli across the street.

"You're in luck. That's one of my favorites."

"Chicken salad?" he asks once we're inside the deli.

"Turkey, swiss, spicy brown mustard, wheat," I rattle off my order.

"Got it. Grab us a seat, beautiful." He kisses me softly before heading toward the counter.

I can feel eyes on us, but I ignore them. I knew going in that being with Jase would garner stares that his fame warrants. I'm not sure if I can deal with the attention, but there is only one way for me to find out. Live it. So, eyes ignored, I grab us a table in the back corner that will hopefully give us a semblance of privacy.

"That was fast," I say when Jase sets our tray filled with our lunch on the table between us.

"Would have been faster had I not had to sign a handful of autographs," he mutters.

"Comes with the job," I remind him.

"I'm retired."

"Maybe, but the damage is done. Besides, I've never known you to not enjoy interacting with your fans."

"Keeping tabs on me, beautiful?"

I shrug. "I've heard you talk about giving back to your fans a few times. It didn't seem as though it bothered you."

"It never used to, but today is different. I'm here with you, and I only get you for an hour. I don't have time for interruptions."

"Yeah, but it's just me. I mean, I knew going into this... whatever we're doing... that you were the infamous Jase Andrews. I know that you come with not only your handsome self but your adoring fans." A look crosses his face, one I can't name, but it disappears when a shadow falls over our table.

"Hi, you're Jase Andrews," a blonde bombshell with her tits on full display says in a husky voice.

"I am," Jase grits.

"I'm Connie." She sways from side to side, waiting for Jase to engage, but he doesn't. "I'm a huge fan. I thought maybe we could get together sometime." She hands him a slip of paper, which I'm certain has her phone number on it, but he just stares at her offered hand.

"I'm in a loving, committed relationship." He points across the table at me. "If you were such an adoring fan, you would respect the fact that the love of my life is sitting across the table from me. Instead, you've disrespected her. I'd appreciate it if you would leave us to enjoy our lunch together."

Her eyes glance my way, and I catch the look of disbelief written on her face. "I could—" she starts but shuts her mouth when Jase stands. Like a train wreck, I can't look away. Her expression changes, and she thinks he's going to leave with her, and I see it written all over her face. My eyes move to Jase, and without a doubt, that's not what's about to happen.

"I've asked you nicely. I won't ask again. Leave us alone." There is fury in his tone, and I know he's about to lose his shit.

I open my mouth to try and calm him down, when Sally, the manager, steps next to the blonde. "Miss, I'm going to have to ask you to order or leave." It looks like Sally has been observing the situation. Not that I'm really all that surprised. She runs a tightly oiled ship, which is part of what makes this place so great.

"Whatever. You're washed up anyway," the blonde hisses at Jase before storming out of the deli.

"I'm sorry," Sally tells us.

"It's not your fault, but we appreciate you intervening," I tell her. She nods and walks away. I glance up at Jase, who looks mad as hell. "Jase," I say his name softly. His eyes snap to mine. "Please sit." He does as I ask, taking his seat across from me. His fisted hands rest on the table. I cover them with my own. "Hey," I say, making sure I have his attention. "Why so angry?"

"It's dumb shit like that, that's going to make me lose you."

His words floor me. "That's why you're so upset?" I ask, needing clarification.

"Jesus, Sam. I just got you. I know my fame is part of why you've kept me at arm's length. If that's what causes me to lose you…" He shakes his head.

"Jase." His eyes snap to mine. "I'm right here."

"For now. How many more times are you willing to deal with that shit?" The anger is replaced by something that looks a lot like worry.

"You told her I was the love of your life," I say stupidly. Not the best time to bring that up, but it's been playing in the back of my mind since the words left his mouth.

He nods.

"I'm going to need more than a nod, player." I use his nickname I've called him for as long as I've known him, hoping to lighten the mood a little.

"I've never been in love before, Samantha. I don't know what it's supposed to feel like. What I do know is that you are all I think about. Something good happens, I want to call you and tell you. If I'm having a shitty day, I think about how it would be to have you coming home to me to share that with. That was all before Friday night. Now…" He shakes his head. "I can't stand to not be near you. I missed you something fierce, and it was with great effort I waited until your lunchtime for me to show up at your office. I can't explain it, and I don't know what it all means." His blue eyes find mine. "It might be love. Whatever it is, I never want it to end."

I take a minute to process his words. "This is how this is going to go," I tell him. He raises his eyebrows but doesn't speak, waiting to see what I'm going to say next. "I want exclusivity. No other women. Just me."

"Done."

"I want lots of your hugs and all of your kisses."

"Done and done." A slow smile crosses his face.

"I want communication. We can't do this… *I* can't do this, live in your world of fame without it. No matter what it is, if it happens, I need to know about it. I don't care if you think it's going to hurt me or upset me. I need to know about it."

"Done."

"Good. Now, eat up. I have to get back to work." I remove my hands from his and pick up my sandwich. I take a bite but can feel his eyes on mine. "What?" I ask once I've swallowed.

"You're mine, Samantha Wilson."

I'm not much for the caveman mantra of "you're mine." I am my own person, but when he says it, I want the words to be true. "You're mine, Jase Andrews," I give his words right back to him.

"Damn right," he says, picking up his sandwich and taking a huge bite.

We finish lunch in record time, and precisely fifty-five minutes later, I'm back at my desk. "Thanks for lunch," I tell him, setting my purse on my desk.

"Can I see you tonight?"

"Yes."

His shoulders relax. "After so long of hearing no, that one simple word is music to my ears."

"I get off at five. I can have dinner ready by six."

"I can bring dinner."

"You need more home-cooked meals. I'll see you at my place at six."

"Can't wait." He leans in for a kiss.

"Get a room," Conrad says, interrupting our moment.

"See you tonight, baby." Jase kisses me one more time. He slaps Conrad on the shoulder and walks away.

"You've bewitched him." Conrad laughs.

"Maybe. I'm not so sure he hasn't bewitched me," I say honestly.

"As long as you're happy, Sam. Jase is a good guy. We all know Royce doesn't like change. He'll get used to the idea. Just give him some time."

"I hope so," I tell him. What I don't say is that Royce needs to be on board because today, at a small deli in Downtown Nashville, I gave Jase Andrews my heart.

CHAPTER FIVE
Jase

"SPEND THE WEEKEND with me," I blurt, just as she's taking a drink of her sweet tea. It's Friday, and we're having lunch together. This time at the pizza place around the corner. I've shown up at her office every day this week to take her to lunch. Royce has grumbled about me stealing his assistant every day, and if it were not for the fact that I crave time with her, I would probably be taking her to lunch just to get a rise out of him.

Tapping her chest, she coughs. "I don't know. I'd have to cancel my plans with Javier."

"Who the fuck is Javier?" I ask, louder than

necessary. My outburst gains me a few stares, but I ignore them.

"He's my hairdresser. I have an appointment tomorrow at ten."

I take in a slow breath and exhale just as slow. "You did that on purpose."

"Maybe." She shrugs.

"I'll drive you to see Javier. Any other plans with any other men I should know about?" I'm only half teasing. My heart dropped when she'd uttered his name.

"No, player. Just you."

"Damn right." I stand and lean over the booth we're sitting in and press my lips to hers—only me.

"I'm off at five," she tells me, which is the only confirmation that I need.

"I'll be at your place when you get there. Pack a bag, and we can go to dinner."

"What if we got takeout instead? Maybe Chinese?" she suggests.

"Done."

"It's been a long week. I'm just ready to chill. Oh, and I have to go grocery shopping and do laundry for next week, so I'll have to head home early Sunday afternoon."

"I'll take you shopping, and we can hang out at your place, and I'll help with laundry and whatever else you need to do. You agreed to all weekend, and I plan to collect."

"Sunday is the end of the weekend."

"No, Monday ends the weekend. We can stay at your place Sunday night if you want." She's stunned if the look on her face is any indication, but that's fine. She'll get used to my need for her soon enough.

"You continue to surprise me."

"How so?" I ask, adding another slice of pizza to my plate.

"I didn't expect you to be so… attentive, among other things."

"Because I'm not. Not usually. I've only ever been this way with you. I never cared enough before to try to put in any effort." It sounds harsh, but it's the facts, and I promised her communication and honesty.

"I always thought you were just being a flirt. All those times you would ask me out, I thought it was a game. I turn you down, and you chase me. You catch me, seduce me, and kick me to the curb."

"I was flirting, I wanted to catch you, and I plan to seduce you." Her eyes smolder at my words. "However, there will be no kicking to the curb. More like tying you to my bed to keep you with me."

Her eyes widen. "You tie a lot of women to your bed?"

"Not to keep them, and never in my bed. Never. The only person who has ever slept in my bed is me. In fact, the only women who have been in my house are my family and extended family. My sister's best friends, Stacy, Lauren, and Cassidy are like sisters to me."

"I bet family functions are full of chaos and good music." She laughs.

"You have no idea. They all keep having kids, and our brood just keeps growing. My mom has adopted all of them. Her list of kids and grandkids is long as hell," I say fondly.

"I always wanted a big family."

"Yeah? How many kids?" I ask her. I'll give her as many as she wants. I'm hoping for a high number. My nieces and nephews have been good training for when I have my own.

"At least two, maybe more. Kids are expensive, so I want to be able to provide for them." She shrugs.

I've got that covered, baby. "We can start with two." For the second time today, she chokes when taking a drink.

"We?"

"You heard me, Samantha." I wink at her.

She tilts her head to the side, studying me. I don't know what she's looking for, but she must find it because a slow smile pulls at her lips. "We can start with two," she agrees.

I want to beat on my chest and shout to the world that this beautiful woman is mine and agreed to give me two babies, but I refrain. Instead, I slide a slice of pizza on her plate. "Eat up, baby. Royce will be shitting bricks if I bring you back late again." I say again because we were two minutes late yesterday. Even though my girl came to work an hour early to work on a project, his broody CEO self was still standing next to her desk, arms crossed over his chest, toe tapping against the tile floor when we got back. I took my time kissing my girl goodbye before blowing a kiss to my best friend. He thinks he's the master of hiding his emotions, but no way could he hide the humor in his eyes.

Royce was crushed by his ex-wife, and now he's suspicious of all women, and all relationships. I hate that bitch for what she did to him. I can only hope that one day a woman will come into his life and change him back to the best friend I lost when his ex tore his world apart. I miss my best friend. He's still here, but he's a shell of the person he used to be. She took away his light.

Maybe when he finds the true love of his life, then he'll understand why I am the way I am with Sam. His marriage was a sham from the start. We all saw it, but he didn't. He had to learn on his own. Sure, we didn't know the extent, but we knew that she wasn't the one for him. Without a doubt, they never should have made it to the altar.

"I'm stuffed," Sam says, pulling me out of my thoughts.

"I guess we need to start heading back," I say, glancing at my watch. "I don't want you getting into trouble."

"Royce is harmless, but yes, I need to get back. I have a busy afternoon. I need to be done at quitting time today. I have big plans this weekend."

"Oh, yeah?"

She nods. "There's this guy. He has these intense,

sexy, blue eyes. He asked me to spend the weekend with him."

I stand and offer her my hand, helping her stand. Once she's on her feet, I pull her into my chest. "Damn right, he did." I kiss her lips. "Let me pay, and I'll walk you back to the office."

CHAPTER SIX
Samantha

AS PROMISED, JASE is sitting in my driveway. I pull my car beside his and grab my purse. "Hey, player." I greet him with a kiss.

"Beautiful," he whispers against my lips. "They're calling for more snow this weekend."

"Okay," I say, not really knowing where he's going with that sliver of information.

"That means I get to be snowed in with you all weekend. We're not going to answer the door or our phones. Just a day of me and you."

"And Javier," I remind him.

He rolls his eyes. "And Javier." I know he's not thrilled to have our time together interrupted, but we can't be attached at the hip. We still have to live our day-to-day lives, and my hair desperately needs a trim.

"Maybe mother nature will be on my side, and Javier will cancel due to the weather."

"This is Tennessee. We're used to snow," I remind him. "You're no longer in Texas."

"A man can dream," he says, following me into my house. "You need any help packing?"

"No, I'm good. Give me five minutes, and I'll be ready to go." I rush down the hall of my small two-bedroom house. It's small, but it's all mine. Sliding open the closet door, I grab a tote bag and begin tossing in clothes. I grab an outfit to change into now, before tossing a couple of pairs of leggings, a hoodie, a sweater, socks, bras, panties, a flannel nightshirt with matching pants to sleep in. I pull my cell phone charger from the wall and toss it in the bag. In the bathroom, I grab my makeup bag before reaching under the sink and grabbing shampoo, conditioner, and body wash—all new bottles. I see a spare loofah and grab that as well. I'll have to restock when I go to the store, but this way I can leave them at his place. I freeze. I can't believe I've so easily fallen into this relationship of ours after going out of my way to avoid the possibility for so long. If I'd had any idea the depth of the man, the extent of what I was missing out on, I never would have denied him.

Going through a mental checklist of what I've

packed so far, I grab a pair of my fuzzy socks that I like to lounge around the house in and call it good. Zipping up the bag, I strip down to my bra and panties to change into some leggings and a sweater. I yelp when I feel hands on my hips. "You sure you don't need me?" Jase's husky voice whispers in my ear.

Staring at my bed, all kinds of naughty thoughts come to mind. Turning in his hold, I wrap my arms around his neck. "I need you." My eyes bore into his, willing him to understand my meaning. I'm not a novice when it comes to sex, but sex with Jase Andrews is, without a doubt, going to be on another level. His body is toned and tight, and I've imagined him hovering over me more times than I can count.

He pushes my hair out of my eyes. "That's not what this weekend is about," he says, catching on to the meaning behind my words. "That's not what we're about. I'm okay with waiting until we're ready. Until you're ready. Whatever it takes to prove to you that I want you. All of you."

"I want you. All of you." I toss his words back at him. Not giving him a chance to stop me, I drop to my knees.

"Fuck, Samantha," he hisses as I make quick work of the button on his jeans, sliding down the zipper, and reaching in, fisting his hard length. "A-Are you trying to kill me?" he asks as I kiss the tip.

I ignore him, happily content to focus on the task at hand. I take him into my mouth. A curse flies from his lips, and his hands find themselves buried in my hair. A thrill races through me at his reaction. I take him deeper this time, before pulling back and repeating the process over and over again.

"Sam," he growls, and before I know what's happening, he takes a step back. I wipe my mouth with the back of my hand while staring up at him. "You're a fucking vision with my cock in your mouth, baby."

"Then why did you stop me?" I was far from finished with him.

"Because I'll be damned if the first time you make me come, it's going to be in your mouth. Come here." He places his hands under my arms and pulls me to my feet. His large calloused hands capture my face, making sure he has my full attention. "You want this? You want me inside you?"

I nod.

"I need your words, Samantha. I need to hear you say it."

"I want this. I want you inside me."

His hands drop from my face, and he reaches into his back pocket. I watch as he fumbles with his wallet, a slew of curses flying from his lips. "Damnit." He tosses his wallet to my bedroom floor. "No condom."

"How is that possible?"

His blue eyes are darker than I've ever seen them. "You. That's how it's possible. The minute I laid eyes on you, you were it for me. It's been almost two years since I've been with anyone."

"Two years? You've only been back for a little over a year," I say, even though he himself already knows this information.

"I gave up playing the field long before I retired, Sam." The look in his eyes conveys his truth.

"I'm on the pill," I blurt. "It's been… longer for me. Going on three years, but I'm clean, and I'm protected."

"You're going to have to spell this shit out for me, Sam. I've never gone bare, baby. Never, and the thought of feeling you with nothing between us—" He shakes his head as his hand grips his cock. "The thought alone has me ready to explode. I need you to tell me what you want. This can end here and now. We'll take your stuff back to my place and start our weekend together."

"I'm saying we're protected. Are you? I mean, have you been tested?"

"Every year. I'm clean, baby."

I nod. "I want you. I want you inside me," I say again.

"Fuck." The world rumbles from deep in his chest. "Strip. I want nothing more than to peel those sexy-as-fuck panties and bra from your perfect body, but I'm ready to lose control. I need you naked, Samantha. Now."

Not needing to be told twice, I jump into action, sliding my panties down my legs, kicking them to the side while reaching behind my back and unsnapping my bra, pushing it down my arms and letting it fall to the floor. "Now what are you going to do with me?" I sass. His eyes heat, and he smirks.

He bends and places his hands on the back of my thighs. "Legs around my waist," he instructs as he lifts me into his arms. "You sure about this?" he asks as his hard cock throbs between us.

"Yes." No hesitation. I trust him.

"Put me in, beautiful."

Needing this ache to go away, I reach between us and grip his cock, rising up and guiding him inside me. "Oh, God," I moan as he fills me.

"Jase," he corrects. "I need to hear you say my name. I need to know that you know it's me inside you."

"Jase," I moan when he pushes all the way in.

"That's my girl," he praises as he turns us and pushes my back against the bedroom wall. "Holy fuck, you're so tight and wet. I-I need to move, Sam. Baby, I want to take my time with you, but fuck, I need to move." His forehead rests against mine, and his chest, much like mine, is rapidly falling and rising with each breath. "I can't—I can't be gentle, not this time. I promise I'll make love to you all weekend, but I'm about to come, and I need you there."

"Take what you need. I need you inside me."

"Hold on, baby."

Not needing to be told twice, my arms tighten around his neck, and I hold on for the ride. Over and over, he slams into me, and the pleasure almost proves to be too much. "J-Jase, I-I can't—" I pant as he continues to slide in and out of me, chasing his own release. Tingles race up my spine, and I begin to squeeze him tight.

"Fuck," he groans, never slowing his pace.

"Jase!" I scream his name as pleasure unlike anything I've ever experienced rolls through my veins like a tidal wave.

"Oh, fuck!" he says as his body stills. I can feel him as he releases inside me, and it's not only intimate, but the realization sends aftershocks through my body. He rests his forehead on my shoulder, and we're both panting. I feel as though I should speak, but words fail me. I don't know that I will ever be able to describe what just happened between us. It was hot, sweaty sex, but it was so much more than that. So. Much. More.

"I'll never be the same," he says, lifting his head. "You hear me, Samantha? I will never be the same." He kisses me softly, a complete contrast to the way he was pumping in and out of me just minutes before.

On shaky legs, he carries us to my bed, and it's not until he has me settled on the mattress that he removes his body from mine. "Let's get you cleaned up and head home. I need you at my place. I need to hold you."

CHAPTER SEVEN
Jase

THIRTY DAYS. THAT'S how much time has passed since the picnic in my living room. I took a chance, and that chance changed my life. *She's* changed my life. Everything is better when I get to share it with Sam. I've seen her every day since the picnic, and all of those days are filled with the feel of her lips pressed against mine, and when I get to hold her, it's as if everything is right in my world.

I told her I wasn't sure what love felt like, but I'm confident now that I do.

Love is Samantha.

My Samantha.

I'm head over heels in love with her and tonight I'm going to tell her.

I had to rally the troops, which is why my mom, sister, and brother-in-law are all standing in my kitchen. "Pulling out the big guns," Kacen says with a nod of approval.

"When do we get to meet her? You've been hiding her from us," my sister, Logan, says.

"You live across the street," I remind her. "She's here all the time."

"I know, but I don't want to come over and see something that will blind me," she teases.

"Well, you've wasted your efforts," I tell her.

Kacen whistles.

"You love her." My mom smiles.

"I do. That's why you're here. I'm going to make us dinner with your help and tell her tonight." My sister pulls me into a hug. "Where are the kids?" I ask her.

"Cole and Stacy took them to the aquarium today."

"Yeah, I was looking forward to some quality time with my wife until you called," Kacen grumbles.

"Oh, hush." Logan waves her hand in the air at him.

"Focus." Mom claps her hands. "We've got work to do."

That's all it takes for us to get busy. I didn't really need Mom and Logan, but how could I ask one and not the other? And Kacen, well, he goes where my sister goes. I used to call him a pussy for it, but it's all making sense to me. One day I'll tell him so, but for now, I need to get busy making homemade beef stew and homemade rolls. Sam once told me that her grandma used to make it when she was little, and she loved it. She said it was one of the comfort foods that always brought back great memories.

I hope tonight is just another memory to add to the list along with those from her childhood. It's fitting since it's the start of the next chapter of her life. At least, I hope she thinks so.

My house smells like a home. That's the first thing I notice when I come downstairs after grabbing a shower. The aroma of the beef stew has my stomach grumbling. I look at the clock and see it's just after four. I'm anxious to see Sam. Last night her best friend Carrie stayed over at her place. Carrie is visiting from San Francisco. She was here yesterday for a meeting and was flying home this afternoon. The plan is for Sam to take her to the airport, then come here. Sam and I had lunch yesterday, but that was the last time I saw her.

The beeping sound of the intercom tells me that someone is coming through the gate. I gave her the code. I want her to have full access to me anytime she wants it. Always.

Heading toward the garage, I hit the opener on my wall. I smile when she pulls into her spot and hit the button to close the door. Cold garage floor be damned as, barefooted, I make my way to her. As soon as she's out of the car, I'm pulling her into my arms. "I missed you."

She chuckles. "I missed you too." She steps out of my hold, closing her door, only to open the back door to retrieve her overnight bag. She doesn't have time to put it on her shoulder before I'm taking it from her hands and leading her into the house. "What smells so good?"

"I made dinner."

"You?" she teases.

"Okay, so Mom and Logan came over and helped me. Kacen too, but he was more of an observer."

"What are we having?"

"Beef stew, salad, and homemade rolls. And," I add before she can comment. "I made a red velvet cake from scratch."

"I'm impressed, player," she says, wrapping her arms around my waist. "I can't believe you made some of my favorites. Again."

"Of course, I did." Dropping a kiss to her temple, I pull away. "I'm going to take your bag upstairs. Salad's made up. Go ahead and start. I'll be right back." I race up the steps and back down to her. She catches me up on her time with Carrie while we eat our salads.

"Oh, God," she moans over her first bite of stew. "This is so good." She takes another bite.

"Right? And I made it. Can you believe that?" I ask, making her smile.

"Your mom and sister are good teachers."

"They want to meet you," I tell her.

She nods. "I'd love to meet them."

"I'll make it happen. I've been selfishly keeping you all to myself, something they made certain to point out to me today."

"My parents said the same thing. In a way, I'm afraid to add in the outside world. I don't want anything to interfere with my time with you."

"I know what you're saying, and I feel the same, but I think it's time we involve our families."

"You do, huh?" she asks.

"It's only fair that I introduce the woman I love to my family."

She freezes. Her eyes widen, and she shoves her empty bowl away from her.

I rake my hands over my face. "I had this big elaborate plan. Dinner, and dessert, and cuddling. I was going to tell you when I had you in my arms, but dammit, I couldn't keep it in any longer. I love you, Samantha."

Tears fill her eyes. "I love you too." She pushes her chair back from the table and comes to stand next to me. Pulling her into my lap, I bury my face in her neck. "I've never felt this way about anyone," I confess.

"Yeah?"

"Life, Samantha. You're stuck with me for life."

"That's not long enough," she mumbles as our lips collide.

Standing with her in my arms, I carry her upstairs and lower her to my bed. "I love you," I whisper, and spend the rest of the night, showing her just how much.

CHAPTER EIGHT
Samantha

JASE AND I are going strong. So strong that we're having dinner with my parents tomorrow night, which leads me to our plans for this evening. Jase thought it was only fair and since he was meeting my family, that I meet his. I've met his sister a time or two, just in passing, but tonight, it's going to be his entire family and extended family. That also means that not only do I meet his parents, but the entire band of Soul Serenade, their wives and kids. Logan, Jase's sister, is married to Kacen Warren, who is the lead singer of Soul Serenade. Only the best freaking rock band to grace the planet.

I'm nervous.

This is more than just meeting the family. His family is full of freaking rock gods. I'm going to make an ass out of myself and that will be the end of us. I know that I'm being dramatic, but come on, it's Soul Serenade for goodness' sake!

"Hey, you ready to head over?" Jase asks.

I've been sitting on his couch freaking the hell out while he grabbed a quick shower. "You sure it's all right if I tag along?" Part of me really wants to go and the nervous part of me thinks I'm better off passing and staying hidden in his house.

"Come here." He offers me his hand and pulls me from my seat on his couch. "I want you with me. I don't care where I am, I want you there. My sister invited us. Not just me, baby. Us. She knows how I feel about you, and she wants you to be there. Besides, my mom has threatened me with no more of her chocolate chip cookies if she doesn't get to meet you soon," he says, kissing the tip of my nose.

"I'm nervous. What if I do or say something to embarrass you?"

"Not possible. I promise you they're just a bunch of goofy guys. All four of them. You've met my sister, and my mom is an older version of her. My dad is just like me. Everyone is laidback. You have nothing to worry about."

"Okay." I nod.

"Good. Grab your coat. We'll walk since it's just down the street, unless you'd rather drive since it's cold out?"

"No, the cold air will do me some good, I think."

"Good." This time his lips meet mine, and I feel some of my nerves melt away.

"Yo! Where's everyone at?" Jase yells as we enter his sister's house without knocking. With his hand clasped around mine, we step further into the house. He doesn't get a reply, but he follows the noise and we end up in the doorway of the living room. There are people and kids everywhere.

"You made it!" Logan, Jase's sister, comes to greet us. "Samantha, it's good to see you again." She leans in for a hug.

"Thank you for having me. Your home is beautiful."

"This is my husband, Kacen." She introduces the man who has wrapped himself around her from behind.

"N-Nice to meet you." I offer him my hand and he takes it.

A throat clearing pulls our attention. Jase, Logan, and Kacen all laugh. "Babe," Jase says. "This is my mom, Beth, and my dad, Jeremy. Mom, Dad, this is my Samantha."

"It's so nice to meet you," his mom says, pulling me into a hug.

"You as well," I say as she releases me.

"Sam." His dad also pulls me into a hug. "Glad to meet you."

"Come on." Logan grabs my hand and pulls me away from her brother. "Come and meet the rest of the gang." I follow along behind her. "Everyone, this is Jase's girlfriend, Samantha. Sam, this is everyone. I'm going to go down the line, but don't worry. We know we're a lot to take on at first."

"All right, those are the kiddos. There are a lot of them, so we'll get to them later." Logan laughs. "This is Cole, and his wife, Stacy." She points to a guy with long hair, who I recognize instantly. They both wave, and we're moving onto the next. "This is Tristan, and his wife, Lauren, and Gavin and his wife, Cassidy." She points out each member of the band and their wives.

"It's nice to meet you," I say to them collectively.

"You'll learn us all," Cole's wife tells me with a kind smile.

"Hey." Jase appears beside me, wrapping me in his arms. "You good?" he whispers just for me.

I turn to look at him and nod, offering him a smile. My nerves are still there, but everyone is so nice and genuine. Not at all what I anticipated meeting guys of their celebrity status.

"Damn." One of the guys laughs. I don't know which one. "Our little Jase has finally fallen." He laughs.

"All it takes is the right woman, brother," Kacen says from his spot beside Logan. Seems like he's with her wherever she is. Although, the way she's snuggled up to his chest, she doesn't seem to mind.

"Grammy, I'm hungry," a little boy who looks just like Kacen says, running up to Jase's mom.

"You heard the boy. Let's eat," Kacen says.

We all file into the huge kitchen, and fill our plates. With each minute that passes, my nerves subside, and I feel like I've known them all for years. We play with the kids, and once they're all tuckered out, the guys break out their guitars and give us a little concert. The entire time Jase has me on his lap, or his arm around me, much like the other guys and their wives. We fit in here. *I* fit in here. Something I never thought I'd be able to say.

CHAPTER NINE
Jase

"ARE YOU NERVOUS?" Sam asks me.

I glance over at her, before placing my eyes back on the road. "No. Should I be?"

She laughs. "I don't know. I was so nervous yesterday to meet your family, and extended family. You have it easy. It's just going to be us and Mom and Dad tonight."

"I want them to like me. But no matter what they think or say, that's not going to change how I feel about you."

"They're going to love you."

"Yeah?"

"Yep. They'll see how happy I am and that's all they care about. You making me happy and being good to me."

"Shit, I've got this in the bag," I tell her.

"Oh, and my dad, he's kind of a fan," she confesses.

"Perfect. If there is anything that I can talk about it's football and you. I should be good."

"I think the last guy my parents met was my prom date senior year of high school."

"Let's not talk about you and other guys, baby."

"I was seventeen." She chuckles.

"I don't care. I'm living in Jaseland where the only man who's ever been on your arm is me."

"Don't you mean the only other arm I've been on?"

"Nope. I'm on your arm and damn proud of it too."

"You keep talking like that and you'll have my parents eating out of the palm of your hand."

"It's not your parents I want, Sam. It's you. I only want you."

"Yeah?"

She's still stuck on my career, and that I'm famous or whatever. I don't know how to show her that she's all I see. Well, I do know how, and I'm hoping tonight will be the night that seals our fate. "None of it matter without someone to share it with, you know that, right? The money, the fame, the accomplishments, the huge-ass house, it's empty without you. And all those other things, they don't mean as much without sharing them." I pull up to the Stop sign and turn to look at her. "I want to share them with you, Samantha. Only you. You make each day brighter and better."

"Sounds like a fairy tale, player," she teases, but I can also hear longing in her voice.

"Then it will be our happy ending," I tell her.

"Turn here." She points to the next street. "Third house on the left." I take her instructions and pull up to a white two-story.

"This where you grew up?"

"Yes. It's also where I brought my prom date." She giggles.

"Samantha," I growl, only making her laugh harder.

"Come on, player. It's time to meet my family." She climbs out of my SUV, and I scramble to pull the keys from the ignition to follow after her.

Much like my sister's house yesterday, she walks inside and calls out, letting them know we're here.

"In the kitchen, sweetheart," a feminine voice calls back.

My Sam smiles up at me and my heart flips in my chest. Now I'm nervous. I know how much she loves her parents, and if they don't approve of me, of us…. Fuck me. Here we go. I follow her into the kitchen, her hand tightly locked in mine.

"Hey," she says, and I can hear the happiness in her voice. "Mom, Dad, this is Jase. Jase, these are my parents, Timothy and Elizabeth."

"It's so nice to meet you." Elizabeth steps around the island and pulls me into a hug. My shoulders relax in her embrace. One down, one to go.

"Jase." Timothy offers me his hand. "It's good to finally meet you."

"You too, sir." I keep eye contact and give his hand a firm shake.

"What are we having?" Sam asks her mom.

"Meatloaf and all the fixings," she says, her Tennessee accent strong. "You three grab yourselves something to drink. Everything is on the table but the rolls. I'll be right there."

"Sweetheart, you want sweet tea?" Timothy asks his wife.

"That would be great. Thank you."

Within minutes, we're all sitting around the table talking and laughing, and I feel right at home. Both of her parents are engaging and I'm not getting any bad vibes. My girl's smile is wide, and that in turn puts me at ease. I love seeing her happy. We move to the living room to chat, and I hope like hell that I have the chance to pull her father aside tonight. If not, I'll have to come back when she's not with me. I know without a doubt she's going to want to know we have their blessing before we take our next adventure together.

CHAPTER TEN
Samantha

"HEY, BOSS, GOT a minute?" I ask, standing in the doorway of Royce's office.

"Sure, what's up?" he asks, giving me his full attention.

"I was hoping I could leave a little early today?" I ask, hopeful.

"Samantha, you don't have to ask. You know that. Just let me know so I'm not looking for you when you're not here," he says. "You and Andrews got big plans for tonight?" he asks.

I nod. "We're going to dinner." Today is

Valentine's Day, our first together, and while I'm excited about it, I'm also worried. That worry comes from something that doesn't even have to do with Valentine's Day. I'm late. As in, my period is five days late. It's only five days, but I'm never late.

Never.

"You all right?" Royce asks.

"Yes." I offer him a smile. "Just excited for tonight."

"Is my best friend treating you right?" he asks.

"You know he is," I tell him with a pointed look.

He holds his hands in the air. "Just making sure. You're good for him," he admits.

"Wait, let me get my phone. I'm going to need you to say that again."

He chuckles. "Smartass. I thought you were leaving?"

"It's only one. I was thinking maybe three or so?" That should give me plenty of time to buy a test or ten, take them, and freak out if I need to. Something deep in my gut tells me I'm going to need the time to freak out and get myself together. I just have this feeling.

"Go now. You never leave early. Enjoy your night with Andrews." He waves me off.

"Thank you. I'll send everyone an email letting them know I'll be gone."

"Sounds good," he says, already returning his focus to whatever it is he's working on.

Making my way to my desk, I type up a quick

email to Owen, Grant, Conrad, and Marshall, letting them know I'll be out of the office and that the elevator will be locked. None of them are expecting a guest, at least none that are scheduled, I already checked. Grabbing my purse and phone, I leave early for the day. First stop, the pharmacy.

Forty-five minutes later, I'm sitting on my bed, staring at ten unopened boxes of pregnancy tests. I grabbed one of every kind and spent a small fortune, but I know me, and one test won't be enough. I'll need further assurance of the results. Reaching for my phone, I dial my best friend.

"Hey, you," she answers.

"Carrie."

"What's wrong?"

"Nothing," I say, barely containing the freak-out mode that wants to take over my body.

"Sam, are you okay? Where's that man of yours?"

"He's at his place, I think."

"Where are you? Samantha, you're scaring me."

"I'm fine, I promise. I just... I'm late."

"Late for what?" she asks, confused.

"No, Carrie. I'm *late*," I say again.

"Oh," she says, as understanding of what I'm trying to say settles in. "Have you taken a test?"

"No, but I bought one. Well, I bought ten."

She laughs. "Of course, you did. Are you alone?"

"Yes. I didn't tell him. I want to take the test first."

"Don't the two of you have plans tonight?"

"We do."

"What time?"

"Six. He's picking me up at six."

"We've got plenty of time. Drink some water, pee on a few sticks, and tell me if I'm going to be an aunt."

"Oh, God. He's going to think I trapped him. He's Jase fucking Andrews, Carrie. How could I let this happen?"

"Jase Andrews is his name. Who he is, is the man that is madly in love with you. From what you've told me, you're both gone for each other. If you are, it's all going to be okay. He's going to be right by your side."

"You don't know that."

"Actually, I do. Put me on speaker and go to his Instagram."

Doing as she says, I place the call on speaker and tap the icon on my phone, and type in his name. He just posted fifteen minutes ago. It's a picture of the two of us lounging on his couch. My eyes scan the caption.

> @JASEANDREWSOFFICIAL—*"Happy Valentine's Day to the love of my life. For those of you who don't know what it feels like to love and to be loved, I feel sorry for you. Take the leap. You won't regret it."*

I don't even attempt to wipe the tears that race down my cheeks. I love him.

"You're crying, aren't you?" Carrie asks.

"Hush," I say, laughing.

"Go pee on a stick or two. I'll wait here."

"I miss you."

"I know. I miss you too, but I'm here for you. Now go."

Doing as she says, I place the phone on the bed, and grab two of the boxes that claim to guarantee early detection. In the bathroom, I carefully unwrap each package and read the instructions. Both are the same. Pee on the stick, replace the cap, wait three to five minutes. Pulling up my big girl panties, well, in this case, I pull them down, with shaking hands, I pee on three different sticks, capping them and placing them on the counter. Finishing my business, I wash my hands and shut the bathroom door.

"I'm back," I tell Carrie.

"Tell me what your plans are for tonight."

"Dinner."

"What if the test is positive?"

"Dinner and an announcement that's going to change our lives."

"For the better. A baby, Sam. You might be having a baby with the man you love. That's amazing."

"And scary as hell," I admit.

"Are you upset? I mean, if the test is positive, are you upset about it?"

"No." I mean it. I might be freaked out, but it's more about how Jase is going to take the news. Sure, we've talked about kids, just briefly, but hypothetical talk is a hell of a lot different than reality.

"He's not going to be either."

"You don't know that."

"I do know that. He has twenty million followers, and he just professed his love for you to all of them. He's going to be fine with it. In fact, I'd go as far as to say that he's going to be thrilled."

"I hope so," I whisper. I know in my heart that she's right, but the fear of the unknown is strong. We've only been together a couple of months. It's too soon.

"Sam, it's time. Take me with you," Carrie says, her voice calm and soothing.

"Here goes nothing," I whisper.

"It's all going to be fine."

I nod, even though she can't see me. Pushing open the bathroom door, I walk to the sink. As soon as I look down and see the word positive, a plus sign, and two pink lines, the tears begin to fall. A sob breaks free from my chest.

"Congrats, sweetie," Carrie says, choking up on her own emotions. "You're going to be a mommy."

"I-I'm going to be a mommy," I echo her words. "I don't know how to tell him."

"You are going to tell him, right?" Carrie questions.

"Yes. I'm going to tell him tonight. He deserves to know."

"You good?" she asks.

"I am," I say truthfully. "Regardless of how tonight turns out, I'm going to be a mom."

"You've got this, Sam, and he's going to be thrilled. Call me with details."

"I will. Thanks, Carrie. I was freaking out."

"What are best friends for?"

Ending the call, an idea pops into my head. Pulling up the internet browser on my phone, I hope like hell I can pull off what I have in mind in just a few hours.

CHAPTER ELEVEN
Jase

THE MOMENT I picked her up, she was acting differently. I don't know if she somehow caught on to my plans for the night, but she's making me nervous.

"Dinner was delicious," Sam says from her seat next to me in my car. "Thank you."

"You're welcome." Reaching over the console, I lace her fingers with mine. "You feeling okay?" I ask her.

"Yes." She's quick to reply. "Fine. Just tired, I guess," she says, and I know she's lying.

Instead of calling her out on it, I let the silence drift between us as I get lost in my thoughts. I realize that I'm terrified that she doesn't want this, doesn't want me. I know that it's soon, but when you know, you know, and if there is anything in this life that's certain, it's the way I feel about her. My love for her.

Pulling into my garage, I shut off the engine. She's staying with me tonight. At least, I hope she still is. "I just need to grab my things from my car. I'll meet you inside," she says, reaching for her handle.

"I can wait for you," I tell her.

"No, really, go on in. That cheesecake needs to be in the fridge," she says, indicating the to-go box full of dessert in my hands from the restaurant. We were both too full to eat it there, so we brought it home. That's playing into my hands perfectly if I could just figure out what's bothering her.

"You sure you don't need any help?" I ask her.

"Promise." She stands on her toes and kisses me on the cheek. "I'll just be a minute."

Heading into the house, I drop the cheesecake off at the fridge and then rush to the living room. Grabbing the ring box from its spot behind a frame on the mantel. I remove the ring and slide it into my pocket. I knew I wanted it to just be the two of us when I asked her. I had to leave it here so that I wouldn't change the course of my plan.

"Come here, you." I hold my arms open for her when she walks into the living room. She doesn't hesitate to come to me as she wraps her arms around my waist. "Where are your things?" I ask her.

"Oh, I left them in the laundry room. I'll grab them before we go to bed."

She usually brings them all the way into the house, and I try not to think too much about it. I'm letting every little action or move stress me the fuck out. I can't wait any longer. The suspense is killing me.

"Do you know how much I love you?" I ask, peering down at her in my arms.

She nods. "I love you too." Her voice cracks.

"Sam." My voice is thick with emotion. "I don't ever want to know what my life looks like without you in it."

"It looks like your past."

I nod. "I only want to look toward the future. I see a wedding, those babies we talked about." I place my hand over her flat belly, and she bites down on her bottom lip. I can see the emotion welling in her eyes. "I want to watch those babies grow and give them a safe place to thrive. I want to sit on a porch swing and watch our babies' babies grow. I want all of that and everything in between. I want the good times and the bad times, and I want the love and the laughter. All of it, I want you by my side." Taking a deep breath, I drop to one knee.

"Wh-What are you doing?" she asks. Her tears are now freely falling from her eyes.

"Samantha Wilson, will you spend your life with me? Will you help me create our future as husband and wife? Will you marry me?" Reaching into my pocket, I pull out the ring and hold it up for her.

"You want to marry me?" she sobs.

"More than anything."

"I-I need to tell you something."

A knot forms in my gut. I knew something was off. "Okay." I can barely speak the word as I climb to my feet and lead us to the couch. "You can tell me anything," I say, steeling my resolve.

"I'll be right back." She stands and takes two steps before turning to look at me. "Don't move." With that, she rushes off toward the laundry room.

My hand is sweating from the fist I have around the ring I just offered her. I don't know what she has to tell me, but nothing could make me change my mind about how I feel about her. Whatever it is, we're going to work it out. Together.

"I got you something," she says, holding a small red bag.

"Babe, I thought we said no gifts?" I ask her.

"You just offered me a ring the size of Texas, is that not a gift?"

"No. It's a promise and a token of how much I love you. Besides, you didn't take it."

"I want to, Jase. I just— You need to hear what I have to say before I take it."

"No." I shake my head. "Forget everything else and tell me. Do you want to be my wife?"

She nods. "More than anything."

Opening up my hand, I reach for her and slide my ring onto her finger. "Will you marry me?"

Her eyes dart to the bag as more tears stream down her cheeks. "Yes."

The word is barely spoken before I'm pressing my lips to hers, wrapping her in a hug so tight I'm sure she's struggling to breathe. "I love you," I say, releasing my iron grip. I cradle her face in my hands. "I love you, and I will no matter what, until the day I take my last breath."

"Open it." She hands me the bag and wipes at her cheeks.

Removing the tissue paper, my hand dives into the bag and pulls out something that feels like jersey material. Holding it up, it's the smallest football jersey I've ever seen. It's dark blue and looks exactly like a mini practice jersey.

"Turn it around."

Turning it around, my name is embroidered on the back. Why is she—? I drop the jersey and lock eyes with her. "What does this mean, Samantha?"

"Keep digging, player." She nods toward the bag.

Reaching into the bag, I feel a small hard object wrapped in tissue paper. Slowly, I unwrap it, not sure of what it is, and what I find has my chest heaving. "We're pregnant?" I say, my voice gravelly.

"Yes, and if you want to take it back, I understand, but I want this baby, Jase."

"Take it back?"

She nods sadly. "The proposal."

"Are you fucking kidding me?" I growl. I toss the test and the jersey to the floor and lean over so that there are mere inches between us. "I want you, and I want this baby. There is nothing in this world I want more. You've made me a husband and a father all in one day."

"Fiancé," she corrects with a blinding smile.

"We're really having a baby?" I ask in awe of the situation.

"Yes. I wasn't sure how you would feel about it. I was so nervous to tell you."

"I could tell something was off, but I never would have guessed that this was the reason. I want this." I place my hand over her heart. "And I want this." I place my hand over her belly. "I love you."

"I love you too."

I hold her in my arms and let the realization wash over me. She made me work for it, but play-by-play, I won her over, and now she's given me two of the greatest gifts. Her heart, and a piece of both of us—a tiny human that we created together. Life doesn't get any better than this.

"Jase?"

"Yeah, baby?"

"You're telling Royce," she says, and we both fall into a fit of laughter.

Never miss a new release:
http://bit.ly/2UW5Xzm

More about Kaylee's books:
http://bit.ly/2CV3hLx

CONTACT Kaylee RYAN

Facebook:
http://bit.ly/2C5DgdF

Instagram:
http://bit.ly/2reBkrV

Reader Group:
http://bit.ly/2o0yWDx

Goodreads:
http://bit.ly/2HodJvx

BookBub:
http://bit.ly/2KulVvH

Website:
www.kayleeryan.com

OTHER WORKS by KAYLEE RYAN

With You Series:
Anywhere With You | More With You | Everything With You

Soul Serenade Series:
Emphatic | Assured | Definite | Insistent

Southern Heart Series:
Southern Pleasure | Southern Desire | Southern Attraction | Southern Devotion

Unexpected Arrivals Series:
Unexpected Reality | Unexpected Fight Unexpected Fall | Unexpected Bond | Unexpected Odds

OTHER WORKS *by* KAYLEE RYAN

Standalone Titles:
Tempting Tatum | Unwrapping Tatum | Levitate
Just Say When | I Just Want You
Reminding Avery | Hey, Whiskey
When Sparks Collide | Pull You Through
Beyond the Bases | Remedy | The Difference
Trust the Push

Co-written with Lacey Black:
It's Not Over | Just Getting Started | Can't Fight It

Cocky Hero Club:
Lucky Bastard

Riggins Brothers Series:
Play by Play | Layer by Layer

ACKNOWLEDGEMENTS

To my family:

Your support means the world to me. Thank you for always standing by my side.

Reggie Deanching:

This image! Thank you for all of your patience as we sifted through galleries of images. I'm excited to finally have one of your images on my covers.

Quinn Biddle:

Thank you for doing what you do. You brought Jase's story to life. Best of luck to you in all of your future endeavors.

Tami Integrity Formatting:

Thank you for making the paperbacks beautiful. You're amazing and I cannot thank you enough for all that you do.

Lori Jackson:

I love this series, and the covers. Thank you for being patient with me, and bringing my vision to life. I can't wait until we reveal the rest of them. Thank you so much for everything.

Lacey Black:

You are my sounding board, and I value that so very much. Thank you for always being there, talking me off the ledge and helping me jump from it when necessary.

My beta team:

Jamie, Stacy, Lauren, Erica, and Franci I would be lost without you. You read my words as much as I do, and I can't tell you what your input and all the time you give means to me. Countless messages and bouncing idea, you ladies keep me sane with the characters are being anything but. Thank you from the bottom of my heart for taking this wild ride with me.

Give Me Books:

With every release, your team works diligently to get my book in the hands of bloggers. I cannot tell you how thankful I am for your services.

Tempting Illustrations:

Thank you for everything. I would be lost without you.

Julie Deaton:

Thank you for giving this book a set of fresh final eyes.

Becky Johnson:

I could not do this without you. Thank you for pushing me, and making me work for it.

Marisa Corvisiero:

Thank you for all that you do. I know I'm not the easiest client. I'm blessed to have you on this journey with me.

Kimberly Ann:

Thank you for organizing and tracking the ARC team. I couldn't do it without you.

Bloggers:

Thank you, doesn't seem like enough. You don't get paid to do what you do. It's from the kindness of your heart and your love of reading that fuels you. Without you, without your pages, your voice, your reviews, spreading the word it would be so much harder if not impossible to get my words in reader's hands. I can't tell you how much your never-ending support means to me. Thank you for being you, thank you for all that you do.

To my Kick Ass Crew:

The name of the group speaks for itself. You ladies truly do KICK ASS! I'm honored to have you on this journey with me. Thank you for reading, sharing, commenting, suggesting, the teasers, the messages all of it. Thank you from the bottom of my heart for all that you do. Your support is everything!

With Love,

Kaylee Ryan
AUTHOR

Made in the USA
Middletown, DE
07 October 2020